Lottie's
Princess Dress

First published in the United States 1999
by Dial Books for Young Readers
A division of Penguin Putnam Inc.
345 Hudson Street
New York, New York 10014

Published in Germany 1998
as *Lotte will Prinzessin sein*
by Ravensburger Buchverlag

Typography by Ann Finnell
Printed in Germany on acid-free paper
First Edition
1 3 5 7 9 10 8 6 4 2

Library of Congress Cataloging in Publication Data
available upon request.

ISBN 0-8037-2388-1

Lottie's Princess Dress

by DORIS DÖRRIE
pictures by JULIA KAERGEL

DIAL BOOKS FOR YOUNG READERS
New York

Lottie's alarm clock buzzed loudly at 7:00 A.M. But Lottie was having a lovely time in dreamland, so she turned it off and closed her eyes again.

"Lottie, honeypie, time to get up," her mother said softly, at ten past seven.

"Not a honeypie," mumbled Lottie without opening her eyes.

"Rise and shine, pumpkin," her mother said a little less softly, "or you'll be late for kindergarten and I'll be late for work."

"Not a pumpkin," Lottie grumbled. "In dreamland I am a princess and I am already at the castle school. We did finger painting and now I am pasting glittery gold things—"

"In wide-awake land," Lottie's mother said in her going-to-work voice, "it's time to get up. Let's see how fast you can get dressed."

Lottie crawled out of bed, followed her mother into the kitchen, and plopped down on the floor.

"I see you got the getting-up part right," said her mother. "Did you forget the getting-dressed part?"

Lottie lay back and stared at the ceiling.

"It's nearly seven-thirty," Lottie's mother said in her no-more-stalling voice. "We're both going to be late if you don't get dressed *right now!*"

"I am thinking about what to wear," said Lottie.

"Put on your blue skirt and red sweater," her mother said.

"No," replied Lottie, "they are too boring."

"Too boring?" her mother asked, looking puzzled. "But last week you told me they were your most favorite clothes!"

"They are not right for today," Lottie said firmly.
"Yes, they are," said her mother, even more firmly.
"GO AND PUT THEM ON!"

Lottie went back to her room. She looked at the red sweater.
It was too red. She looked at the blue skirt. It was too blue.
Then she saw her princess dress. It was glittery gold
and it was perfect!

Lottie fixed her hair in a princess style. Then she called to her mother, "I am getting dressed now."

"I'd better come and help," her mother replied.

"Oh, no!" said her mother when she saw Lottie.
"Why aren't you wearing your blue skirt and red sweater?"
    "Today is a glittery gold day," said Lottie.
    "Today is a freezing cold day," said her mother,
"much too cold for that dress."
    "It is not," said Lottie.
    "It is too!" her mother insisted.
"Go out on the balcony and see for yourself."

"I see snowflakes," announced Lottie's mother.

"You must be dreaming," said Lottie. "They are g-g-glittery gold spots of s-s-s-sunshine."

"Am I also dreaming that your teeth are chattering?" asked her mother. "Now come inside, and put on something sensible."

"My princess dress is perfect for today," Lottie said crossly.

"Princess dresses are for special days, like Halloween,"
Lottie's mother said in her don't-even-think-about-arguing voice.

"A glittery gold day *is* special," Lottie argued.

Her mother's face turned bright pink.

"Lottie Van Klinkenstopper, you are making us late!"
she said quite loudly. "March into your room
and put on your blue skirt and red sweater, or
I'll ... I'll ... I'LL HAVE A TANTRUM RIGHT NOW!"

"You are too big for tantrums," replied Lottie, because that
is what her mother always said if Lottie started to have one.
"I AM NOT!" said her mother.
And, to Lottie's surprise, she wasn't!

"Wow!" said Lottie. "You looked like a dragon. I am glad I remembered that princesses are not afraid of dragons."

"And I'm sorry I forgot that tantrums don't work," said Lottie's mother, "for me *or* for you!"

"Can I still wear my princess dress?" Lottie asked.

"Honeypie, you're making me crazy today."
Lottie's mother sighed. "Well, maybe if you
wore your warm coat . . ."

"Hooray!" shouted Lottie. "I will polish
my crown."

Lottie's mother laughed. "How about brushing
your teeth instead?"

While Lottie brushed, she watched her mother in the mirror.
"Your clothes are not right for today, Mom," Lottie said.

"And what should I wear, Your Highness?"
her mother asked.

"Red dress with glittery gold spots," Lottie gurgled through
toothpaste foam.

"But, Lottie, that's an evening dress," her mother said.

"Does that mean you can only wear it at night?"
asked Lottie.

"Well, no, but it's only for special occasions," Lottie's mother explained.

"Today *is* special," Lottie exclaimed, "and you will look like a beautiful queen!"

"Hmmmmm . . ." said her mother, looking at herself in the mirror.

"Please, Mom?" Lottie asked in her very nicest voice.

"Are you ready for school, Princess Lottie?" her mother asked.

"Yes, Queen Mom," said Lottie happily. "I think we look perfectly special."

"We most certainly do!" Lottie's mother agreed.

"You can borrow my extra crown," said Lottie.
"It is too big for me."

Lottie and her mother walked to the bus stop. It wasn't snowing anymore, and their glittery gold dresses kept them as warm as summer sunshine.

"Oooh!" said one woman as they passed by. "Today must be a very special day!"

"Where may I take your highnesses today?" the bus driver asked.
"To kindergarten," replied Lottie.
"And to work," her mother added.

At work everyone told Lottie's mother how special she looked.
"You should see my daughter," she said happily.

At school Lottie and her best friend made up a story about a king,
a magic carpet, and a princess in a glittery gold dress.
Everyone agreed it was a perfectly special day.

DORIS DÖRRIE is a film director and screenwriter. She also writes novels and short stories for adults. *Lottie's Princess Dress* is her first book for children. It was inspired by her daughter, Carla, who sometimes can't decide what to wear in the morning. Ms. Dörrie and Carla both enjoy wearing princess dresses.

JULIA KAERGEL is an artist whose work has been exhibited in many countries. This is her first children's book. When she isn't painting, Ms. Kaergel enjoys riding her bicycle and going canoeing. She also enjoys wearing her princess dress and crown.